THE VAMPIRE'S VISION

SHAWN WISEMAN

TABLE OF CONTENTS

1. TWO BITES ARE BETTER THAN ONE

*K*ara checked her phone again. *She's late*, she thought. *As usual.*

The cold autumn air flew past Kara in a streak, and she shivered as it stole the heat from her body. She used her ability to shield herself from the cold wind. The air arched its way around her this time, and then went off without bothering her again.

Genetic lottery paying off again. She chuckled at her own joke.

Winter was on its way, but Kara already couldn't wait until it was over. The cold always hurt her teeth and made her skin dry. The only part she liked was that the sun, reaching its noonday peak, wasn't as strong, so she at least wouldn't have to worry about sunscreen and burns.

Kara looked up and down the sidewalk, and saw Olivia walking to meet her. Kara waved with a smile, and Olivia waved back fervently.

Olivia was wearing jeans, a tank top, and a thin jacket despite the cold. Somehow Olivia was even able to make her ivory skin look normal against the color of her clothes and straight, chestnut brown hair. *That's attention to detail, I suppose.* Kara always liked what Olivia wore, but could never pull it off. Comfortable jeans and a hoodie was her choice of fashion, trendiness be damned.

"Kara!" Olivia shouted. As she approached she went to give Kara a hug, but her face stopped as it hit an invisible barrier. She pulled back and blurted out an "ouch" as she rubbed her face, even though Kara knew it hadn't hurt her.

"Sorry, Liv." Kara closed her eyes and relaxed her mind to dissipate the barrier. "I was cold."

Olivia's eyes widened. "Oh, yeah. That is a nifty trick. I wish I could do that, maybe then I wouldn't have to brush my hair every time the wind blew."

Kara chuckled. "You're late to your own meeting, again."

Olivia had a worried look on her face. "I know, I'm sorry. You know how much of a ditz I am." She touched Kara's arm. "Can you forgive me?"

Kara rolled her eyes. "I always do… So, what's so urgent, Liv? Did you just miss me?" she asked, pouting her lips.

Olivia laughed. "No, I need your help with something."

Kara's smile faded, and she sighed. "You know I know what you want help with, right?"

Olivia's face became stern. "I know."

"And you know I don't like helping you with that, right?"

"I know."

"And you know you're just using me because you know that I'm going to help you despite my protesting, right?"

"I know, Kara. It's just… I feel a lot safer with you there. At least for these types of jobs."

Kara sighed again, but there was a slight smile in the corner of her lips. "So, who's the deadbeat this time?"

"James Moore," Olivia replied. "He owes the boss for his vices, as usual. He lives in that building." Olivia pointed to a building down the street.

"Lead the way," Kara said, putting her hood up and her hands in her pockets.

Olivia took the lead and went inside the building where her mark lived. The elevator was busted, so they took the stairs to the third floor. When they reached the top of the stairs, Olivia stopped to put her hair in a ponytail.

"Are things going to get that serious?" Kara asked.

"Always helps to be prepared, and he owes a lot of money. How are my teeth?" Olivia flashed her white smile, showing off her long incisors.

"Perfect, as always," Kara replied. "How about mine?" Kara did the same as Olivia, showing off her not so perfect white teeth and pointed fangs.

"Sharp," Olivia commented before she turned around and went into the hallway of apartments. "Did you use those strips I gave you?"

Kara followed Olivia through the dank, dingy, and smelly hallway. "They hurt my teeth. So, no."

"It's a shame, you have such nice fangs too. Not that you use them much."

"Thanks, I think."

"Well, you're half vampire, you should act the part. You can't rely on the dead your whole life."

Kara frowned. "I'm a full vampire as well as a psychic, Liv. You know I don't like being called that."

Olivia turned around in front of one of the apartment doors. "I'm sorry. You know I didn't mean it like that."

Kara nodded, but it still stung. "Is this the place?"

"Yeah, this is it. Ready?" Kara nodded, and Olivia knocked on the door.

There was no answer. Olivia knocked again, louder than before. Kara could hear some shuffling from inside the home. She tensed her mind, getting ready for what could happen next.

"Who… who's there?" a sleepy voice asked.

"We have a pickup for Mr. Green," Olivia replied.

There was a pause. "Does Mr. Green bring cash?"

"Of course."

The lock on the door clicked, and the door opened. A man in his late twenties stood before them. He had bags under his eyes, a shaggy, unkempt beard, and a rank smell. Kara presumed this was the James Moore they were looking for.

"Welcome, ladies," he said in a sick, flirting tone.

Kara and Olivia entered his house, which looked as expected, though a bit cleaner than Kara had thought it would be. There was a severe lack of furniture—only a couch, a cluttered coffee table, a large, new-looking TV, and a decent-looking computer in the corner. The blinds were closed, so what little light could enter was shrouded. Dirty dishes were piled in the sink, but the tables and counters were clear.

3

Smoke permeated the air like a permanent resident, and it was unclear where it came from, or how long it had lingered.

Kara went to the couch and put her feet up on the coffee table between an ashtray and a bong on one side and a TV remote on the other. Inwardly she was disgusted, but outwardly she carried an air of indifference to mask their charade.

"What's the damage?" Olivia asked.

James closed and locked the door. He had several locks, so it took a moment. "First, you guys aren't cops, are you?"

Olivia raised her eyebrow, and put her hand on her hip. "Do we look like cops?"

James glanced from Olivia with her stone-cold-fox air of superiority over to Kara's lackadaisical lounging on his couch. He nodded in what seemed to be approval. "Andy'll get you an ounce."

"Give me three then." Olivia took her wallet out of her jacket and pulled out three twenties to hand to James. He took them without hesitation and with a cringe-worthy smile on his face.

James whistled. "I'll be right back, ladies."

He vanished to the back of the apartment. Kara got up, and she and Olivia followed James without making a sound. They sneaked up to the doorway of the room he entered and peered inside. Kara saw James kneeling down in front of a closet, and punching in a combination for what appeared to be a small safe. James glanced over his shoulder. With her superior reflexes, Olivia managed to pull Kara away in time.

Olivia motioned for them to return to the living room. After another moment, James entered the living room with a plastic bag in his hands.

Kara motioned for James to give her the bag. "Liv, can I just take a hit before we get going?"

Olivia nodded to Kara. Kara opened the bag and took a little bit of the weed out, then placed it in the bong on the coffee table. She grabbed a lighter and inhaled the smoke accumulating in the bong, then sat back and blew it out, letting it join with the smoke already in the room.

"You good?"

The Vampire's Vision

Kara coughed, and then laughed. "Oh, yeah, I'm good." Kara focussed her mind through the fog the drug created, and she was ready.

Olivia smiled, showing her fangs to James. His face contorted in confusion before he quickly seemed to realise what was happening. He threw his arms up and furrowed his brow, but nothing happened, which confused him even further.

Olivia grabbed him, swept his leg, and threw him to the floor. She opened her mouth, showing off her fangs in a threatening manner, and pinned him to the floor by sitting on his waist.

James let out a small scream of terror and pulled his face back. "Is this about the money I owe to Vasha? I swear I'll have it all by next week. Please, please don't kill me."

Olivia snarled, eliciting another yelp from James. "Vasha's tired of waiting. We know you have money, we saw the safe. Give me the combination and make this easy, otherwise..." Olivia flashed forward and touched the skin of James's neck with her teeth. "I'm going to take out my frustrations on you."

Kara had to concentrate on James throughout the whole interaction. She could feel the shiver going up his spine when Olivia's hot breath caressed his skin. He was pushing against Kara's bonds, and wasn't willing to take their assault lying down. If it wasn't for her countering his abilities, Olivia would be in real trouble. Despite his looks he was a decently powerful psychic.

James looked at Olivia, then over at Kara as sweat beaded on his temples and fell to the carpet below. "Alright, alright. It's twenty-three, fifty-eight, two."

Olivia pulled herself up, but kept James pinned. "What do you think? Is he being cooperative?"

Subconsciously, Kara had begun leaning forward and maintaining strict eye-contact with James during the whole conversation. "He was being testy, but now he seems docile."

"You alright to handle things here while I open the safe?"

"I'll be fine."

Outside the apartment, the sound of several police sirens came blaring within earshot and settled in front of the apartment. All three sets of eyes moved to the window covered by the blind, where the faint glow of red and blue flashed through the crack in the centre every second.

Olivia looked at Kara with concern. She got up off of James and went to the window to peek outside. She could see police exiting the vehicle and entering the apartment building.

"I'll be right back, hold him there," Olivia said.

"Do you think they're coming here?" Kara asked to Olivia's back.

"Better not to be here if they are," she replied as she rounded a corner into bedroom hallway.

Kara kept her mind focussed on James as she walked backwards to the window to look outside.

"I never thought I'd see a psychic working with a filthy vampire."

Kara turned her head around and gritted her teeth. She slammed James' head on the carpet. "Shut up," she commanded.

James' face twisted in pain as he eyed Kara from afar. He did a double take. "Wait a minute, I know you. You're the freak. A vampire *and* a psychic."

Kara frowned. "You know, for having no power in this situation you're really pushing your luck."

"Dirty half-breed. I hope the cops do come here. I know some detectives who have it out for vampires."

Kara slammed his head against the floor again. "It's genetics, asshole. We're all the same, we just have different abilities. I just happened to win the fucking lottery." *A shitty lottery.*

Olivia came back into the living room. At the same time, there was a sharp knock on the door.

"Police, open up."

Olivia motioned for Kara to come with her.

"Help! I'm being held hostage!" James yelled.

Olivia's and Kara's eyes widened. Olivia jumped on James and punched him in the head, knocking him unconscious.

The police started trying to kick the door down. The locks were giving them trouble, which meant there was more time for Olivia and Kara to escape. They ran to the bedroom hallway, where there was a large window which opened to a fire escape. The banging got louder, and there was a crack as the frame on the door started to buckle. Olivia opened the window and pushed Kara out.

The Vampire's Vision

Kara climbed up to the edge of the window and shuffled through the opening. She turned around on her knees to help Olivia just as the noise of footsteps and a "Clear!" could be heard behind them. Olivia was in the middle of exiting the window. She put her hands under Kara's knees and, with her superior strength, she tossed her friend over the side of the fire escape.

Kara could barely register what had happened before she was halfway to the ground from a three-storey drop. She strained her thoughts and slowed her fall before she hit the ground, then she rolled on the street.

Kara hurried to her feet and turned around to see her best friend dragged back into the apartment by police. Kara panicked as millions of thoughts rushed through her head, all variations of concern for Olivia over what James had said about psychic detectives. The cold wind felt like nothing; her thoughts were elsewhere.

After a few moments, the police came out of the apartment building carrying James and pushing Olivia into the squad car with her hands cuffed behind her back. A few passersby stopped to watch the scene.

Kara frowned and started to use her powers, but she saw Olivia's face. She was shaking her head back and forth, telling Kara not to do what she was about to do.

Kara could only stand there as they took her friend away into unknown   dangers.

7

2. VASHA, THE WOMAN WHO NEVER DIED

*K*ara exited the cab in front of the local precinct of the police. She looked at the front of the stone building, with its high walls and many plain windows and features. *Please be safe, Olivia.*

Kara entered the precinct. Inside was a spacious room with wooden benches near the entrance and hallways on either side. In front of her was a small line of people waiting to be served at the front desk, where a few uniformed officers were helping them.

Kara had to wait in line, and it was killing her. It was slow-moving, and it was noisy. Every minute that passed she kept thinking Olivia was in trouble. She took out her phone and texted Olivia on the off chance that she'd been released before Kara got there.

Where are you, Liv? She kept it light in case someone else had access to Olivia's phone.

When Kara looked up, she was at the front of the line. She was soon called over to one of the officers at the front desk.

"Hello, I'm looking for a friend who was… picked up recently."

The officer nodded. "Can I have their name, please?"

"Olivia Lucero."

The Vampire's Vision

The officer typed the name into his computer, clicked a few times, and then shook his head. "No one going by that name has been brought in."

The news stunned Kara. "Uh, what about any unnamed women within the last half hour?"

The officer scrunched his mouth while looking at the computer. "Hmm." After a few clicks, the officer shook his head again. "No, I'm sorry. No Jane Doe brought in within the last half hour."

Kara's face fell. "Thank you," she mumbled as she shambled out of the police station.

Where could she be? Unless… She turned and looked back at the police precinct. *They're hiding her in there? Was what James said the truth? Are there detectives who are psychics?* Kara could sense psychic energy emanating from all around the police station, but she couldn't tell who it was, or how many people it was coming from. It could be civilians, criminals, or it could very well be the police. She shook her head and stormed off, not knowing what to do.

Kara took a cab back to her home, a small apartment building in a poor part of town that she shared with an old man she took care of. When she turned the key in the lock and opened the door, a familiar voice greeted her.

"Who's there?" the old man yelled.

"It's just me, Mr. Montgomery."

Magnus Montgomery turned in his recliner to better look at Kara as she took off her hoodie and revealed her face. "Where were you? You look like shit."

Kara wiped her eyes. "Out with a friend." She took out her phone and checked for texts.

Magnus nodded with a raised brow. After a moment, he turned back in his recliner and resumed watching television. "You gonna make me something to eat? It's lunchtime."

Kara was still looking at her phone, and then she let out a sigh and put the phone back in her pocket. "Yes, I'll have something ready in a bit."

"Put some more meat in it this time," Magnus demanded.

"The doctor said that you shouldn't be eating so much meat," Kara said as she took some things out of the fridge to cook with.

"I don't care what the doctor said. I want more."

Kara smiled and continued cooking, glad for the distraction. It gave her enough time to clear her head, but it still didn't provide her insight on what she should do next. Before she knew it she was eating at the table with Magnus.

"…with you?"

Kara came out of her thoughts with the sound of Magnus' voice. "I'm sorry, what?"

"I said what's wrong with you, girl? You've been in space since you walked through the door."

Kara paused for a moment, considering whether she should tell Mr. Montgomery or not.

"Spill it out, Kara." It was one of the few times Magnus used her first name, and she knew he meant business, but underlying it all was genuine concern.

"A friend of mine got into some trouble at her job, and now I don't know what to do to help her. I don't know where she is, and she's not responding to her texts."

"Is it that bitch, Olivia?"

Kara frowned. "Don't call her that! She's not a bitch, and the only reason she lashed out at you that time was because you harassed her."

Magnus shrugged his shoulders. "If she didn't have such a nice tush I wouldn't want to give it a squeeze." Kara sighed. There was no changing Mr. Montgomery. After a moment he took on a serious tone. "She's strong. She'll be alright."

Kara peered at Magnus, but he was staring at his food. For a moment, she felt that he was right. Olivia was strong, and more often than not she was helping Kara instead of the other way around. But then Kara remembered what James had said about there being psychics within the police force. Olivia couldn't do anything about psychics, and if they found out she was a vampire, then there's no way she would leave the station unscathed.

"If you're that concerned about her, why not talk to her employer? Maybe they can help you out."

Kara hadn't thought of that. Olivia's employer, Vasha, had connections and could pull some strings to find out where she was. And, if she was being held in the police station, she might even be able to get her out. Kara had misgivings about meeting with Vasha, but it was her best bet at the moment.

The Vampire's Vision

Kara got up from the table and gathered her things. "Thanks, Mr. Mongomery. I'll be back later."

"Stay safe," Magnus said, not turning around.

"I will," Kara replied as she exited the apartment.

She pulled out a business card from her wallet. On the front in a stylized font was the name *Vasha*, and on the back an address. The font was ostentatious at best, and even though Kara had never met Vasha before, from this and from what she'd heard of the woman, she was in for a ride.

Kara hailed a cab to take her to Vasha's address, but when she stepped out in front of an Italian restaurant she became confused. She leaned into the window of the cab.

"This is the place?" she asked while pointed to the restaurant. The cabbie confirmed that it was the correct address, and then sped off for a new fare.

Kara shrugged her shoulders and entered the restaurant. As soon as she opened the door the smells coming from the kitchen filled Kara's nostrils with intoxicating sweet and savoury notes. Inside, the small restaurant was cleanly divided into sections. On the left was a bar with stools lining the counter, and a hefty stock of alcohol. There were a few patrons drinking and talking with each other at the bar, despite it being the afternoon. On the middle and right side of the restaurant there were tables and booths for a fine dining experience. And finally, at the back, there was the chef's table in front of an open kitchen.

In front of the chef's table there were two large men acting as bodyguards for a woman currently eating at said table. The bodyguards fixed their eyes on Kara the minute she walked in, and despite their relaxed appearance, she could tell they were like coiled snakes: ready to strike at a moment's notice.

Seriously? What is this, a gangster movie?

She walked over to the chef's table, completely indifferent to how she looked in what appeared to be a classy restaurant. The bodyguards tensed and one of them put their hand out to stop her.

"No entry beyond this point, miss."

"I'm here to see Vasha," Kara replied. She tried to look behind the guards to whom she thought was Vasha, but the guards tightened their formation and blocked her view.

"Make an appointment," the other guard commanded.

I don't have time for this. Kara tensed and used her mind to bind the guards, and then she passed by them unimpeded. She sat down at the chef's table in front of Vasha.

The woman had the palest skin Kara had ever seen, almost as if she were a marble statue come to life. The left side of her jet black hair was partially shaved, and the rest flowed in waves over her right shoulder and rested on her chest. A ruby hairpin held it in place so it wouldn't fall on her face as she moved, and she wore an opulent necklace and several rings on her fingers. She was tall and lithe like an athlete, and yet from her lips, chest, and hips she was voluptuously figured. She was wearing a pin-stripe suit which somehow showed off her curves and gave her a powerful yet provocative look. Men and women alike would no doubt be drawn to her beauty.

Kara couldn't help but stare at her. Olivia had mentioned how beautiful Vasha was, but this was on a whole other level.

"And you are?" Vasha asked, but the tone was more like a command. She didn't even feel the need to look up from her food to acknowledge Kara was there, despite hearing the exchange with her bodyguards.

"I'm Kara. Are you Vasha?"

"Of course I am," Vasha quipped

"Of course you are," Kara repeated, feeling as small as an ant.

"Olivia's mentioned you. You're quite unique. A psychic and a vampire, how… interesting."

Kara couldn't help but gulp at Vasha's tone of pure ecstasy. It was as if, in that instant, Vasha was draining her blood and drinking in her essence. Kara reached for her neck just to be sure there weren't any marks.

Vasha finished her meal, wiped her mouth, and then glared at Kara. Her mind went numb and she felt like she'd lost something. Before she could recover, the body guards had their powerful arms on her.

"Leave her," Vasha commanded.

"Yes, Miss Vasha." The guards removed their hands from Kara and went back to their post without any deliberation.

Kara was sweating, and she knew better than before that she was in the presence of an unbelievably powerful vampire. "How…?" was all she could muster.

12

The Vampire's Vision

"When you've lived as long as I have, my dear," Vasha began, picking up a wine glass with a red, viscous liquid in it, "you learn a few tricks."

Kara knew what the drink was. Its intoxicating smell was swimming in the air, dancing on her nose and tempting her with its nostalgic taste. It had been so long since she'd fed, and the sweet nectar's aroma made her weak in the knees with anticipation. She needed to remain strong. Now wasn't the time for that.

Vasha took a drink from the glass, and Kara could see her perfect white teeth and long fangs. "Why are you here? Speak up, now."

Kara cleared her throat. "Olivia was at the job you sent her on when police showed up and took her away. I went to the station the car was from and they didn't have any record of her arriving, nor any women in the timeframe which she should have arrived in. She's also not replying to any texts I've sent."

"That's a problem... but I don't see what it has to do with me."

Kara's jaw dropped, and despite the numbness that the woman's gaze gave her, she became angry. "It *is* your problem. She works for you. You need to help her get out of whatever trouble she's in!"

"No, I don't *need* to do anything, actually. It is my choice when I perform any action, and I don't see any reason to act at this time."

"The man you wanted her to get the money from, he said there are other psychics in the police force, detectives, and that he would tell them that she's a vampire. If they find out about her, they'll hurt her."

"Oh my, how tragic," Vasha replied, taking another sip of her drink.

Kara gritted her teeth in fury. "What's wrong with you! Olivia talks so highly of you, but you won't even help her."

Vasha held her hand up, silencing Kara. "I gain nothing by doing what you ask. If she is indeed in police custody, and they are aware of her race, I only bring unwanted attention to myself by announcing our mutual association. Olivia is special, she will make it out on her own. And, if she doesn't, there will be others to replace her."

Kara fumed, but before she could lash out, Vasha spoke again.

"I suppose I could be convinced to lend my aid."

Kara's anger subsided a twinge. "How?"

"If I was offered the favour of one psychic vampire for use at my discretion, why, that would be quite the bargaining chip indeed."

13

"Tch." Kara shook her head and looked away from Vasha as she considered the proposition. "What kind of favour?"

"Indiscriminate. When I have use of your particular services, I will call, and you will answer. No questions asked." Vasha emphasised each word with deeper inflection.

Kara's thoughts drifted to Olivia and what might be happening to her right now. She had heard about horror stories of what psychics have done to vampires in the past, seen them first-hand even, and the thought brought chills to her spine. She was desperate and didn't know where else to turn at this point.

"Alright, please just help however you can."

Vasha smiled in a way that made Kara sick. "Excellent. I shall apply some pressure and I'll let you know what I find. And don't worry, I already have your number."

Kara got up from the chef's table and began to leave, but stopped just short of the bodyguards. She looked over her shoulder and said, "You know, the whole gangster thing is really cliché."

Vasha laughed as she lifted her wine glass in one hand and folded her arms. "What can I say? I liked the fifties."

3. THE NEED TO FEED

*K*ara walked down the street, the cold wind once more blowing in her face. She was too focussed to even take the time to stop the gust with a psychic barrier. She might not have the contacts that Vasha had, but she knew people who knew people.

She went up to an old dilapidated house in what police called a "bad neighbourhood." She knocked on the door and then shoved her hands back into the pockets of her hoodie. She could hear music playing inside the house, so there were definitely people home. She knocked again after a moment.

Soon, someone opened the door. In front of her was a muscular and tall man from the same generation as she. He had the chiselled features of an Adonis from the modern age, the alabaster skin of an aged-as-wine vampire, and the look of a pissed-off bulldog aimed straight at Kara.

Of course it had to be him.

"What are you doing here?" he questioned, crossing his arms.

"Nice to see you again too, Damien," Kara replied with a smile. "I'm here to see Raymond."

"Yeah, I'll bet. Nobody wants you here, so why don't you just—"

"Kara?" a soft voice called from further into the house.

Kara smiled. "Hi Raymond."

Raymond came over and glanced back and forth between Kara and Damien, unsure of what to do. He was like an antithesis to Damien. He was short but wiry, wore glasses, and had bags under his eyes. He had the same white skin as Damien, but on Raymond it felt more like aged vinegar than wine.

"Ignore him," Kara said, pulling Raymond between her and Damien. Damien refused to leave though, even after her display. "Did you get my text? Did you find out anything?"

Raymond nodded. "No specifics, but I did hear a rumour going around about a lot of psychics being detectives. It's easy to catch people when you can read their minds. Makes them look like better detectives because they can close more cases." Raymond chuckled.

"And what about..." Kara glared at Damien, hesitant to say Olivia's name in front of him.

"Olivia?" Raymond finished.

Kara let out a sigh at Raymond's gaffe. The look on Damien's face changed from anger to concern in an instant.

"What's wrong? Is Olivia in trouble?"

Kara pursed her lips and grabbed Raymond's arm. She took him outside, over the threshold of the house, and put up a barrier. Damien tried to follow, but was stopped in his tracks.

"You still have a car?" she asked.

"Yeah," Raymond replied.

Kara walked to the side of the house, pulling Raymond along. Raymond entered one of the vehicles in the driveway, and she entered the passenger seat.

"Where do you want to go?"

"Away."

Raymond nodded, turned on the car, and drove it away from the house. He drove to a nearby park which was nearly empty save a few couples walking hand in hand and an old man feeding birds that had yet to migrate.

"So, what happened to Olivia?"

"I wasn't able to find that out, but I did find out that police picked up a vampire and are holding whoever it is in the precinct you mentioned. It wasn't on any official channels though, so it could be a rumour."

"No, that's Olivia for sure. The timing is too close to be a coincidence." Now that Kara had confirmation Olivia was being held in the police station, she just needed to wait for Vasha to pull through. She let out a sigh. At least she knew where Olivia was now. All that was left was to get her out of there.

Kara felt a sharp pain begin at the back of her head and creep to the sides. She thought it might have been the pressure and stress, but she knew it was something else. Her teeth ached and she felt tired. She held her head and began taking deep breaths.

"You haven't fed in a long time, have you?" Kara shook her head. "You need something." Raymond reached into his pocket and pulled out a twist-off vial carrying a red liquid. "Here, take mine. It's from a blood bank one of the guys raided."

Kara looked at the vial with longing. The blood called to her as her brain pulsated and pounded. It would be so easy to take Raymond's offer and ease the pain, but she refused. That was a road she didn't want to go down again.

"Still feeding on the recently deceased?"

Kara nodded, trying to push the fatigue and the headache away. If not for Vasha's drink that had smelled so intoxicating, she wouldn't be feeling this right now.

"You always were a woman of conviction," Raymond said with a slight chuckle.

Kara couldn't help but think he wanted to say more than he did. "But you think it'll end up killing me one day, huh?"

Raymond's eyes went wide. She'd hit the stake in the heart. "Don't worry, I can't read minds. It was just obvious what you wanted to say."

Raymond nodded, his expression changing to concern. "I just don't want you to die, Kara. Those other guys just don't understand, but someday they'll come around."

"I don't want to wait a few generations for that to happen," Kara replied, rubbing her neck and temples.

"Well, I think you're really cool." Kara glanced over at Raymond and he shook his head. "I… I mean your powers." He took a few breaths and wiped his brow. "I think it would be awesome to be able to move things with your mind, or read other people's minds."

"I think if you were the one who had this *blessing* you'd think differently. Although, having the power to read people's minds could come in handy. I wish I had that. Maybe then I wouldn't have to do all this running around."

"Well, telekinesis is still pretty cool, and what was it you called that other thing… where you can see people before they die?"

"Death Knell."

Raymond chuckled. "For whom the bell tolls, huh?"

"Exactly," Kara replied with a smile. The headache wasn't gone, but it had subsided a bit. She leaned over and hugged Raymond. "Thank you Ray, you've always been there when I needed you, and I haven't been a good friend to you."

Raymond pulled away from Kara and shook his head vigorously. "Don't say that. I know why you don't come around anymore…" He trailed off, not wanted to bring up old wounds, or retread fresh ones received from Damien. "I could try harder, if it wasn't for all the crowds."

Kara had a sad smile on her face. "Tell you what, when all this is over, let's all go to that restaurant you like."

Raymond laughed. "The one with the horrible food?"

Kara nodded. "At least there we don't have to worry about crowds."

"True that," Raymond said with a smile.

Kara gave Raymond another hug, said her goodbye, and left the car. She waved to him as he drove back to the house where he, Damien, and the others lived.

She could feel the pang of hunger and the desire to bite someone's neck open. The couples in the park were tempting, but Kara meditated for a moment and the pang was gone. She needed to focus.

She pulled out her phone and texted the number on Vasha's business card. She asked if there was any further information on Olivia, as she had been able to confirm she was with the police.

After a moment, she received a reply, but it was a generic text about Vasha's restaurant saying that it can't accept texts. *Of course she wouldn't put her real number on the business card.* Despite that, after another moment passed, she received another text from a different number saying to come to the restaurant.

She rode a cab back to the restaurant, lamenting the fares she'd had to pay over the course of the day. *When this is over, Liv, you're treating me and Ray to that meal.*

The Vampire's Vision

She went into the restaurant and to the back, where Vasha was still sitting at the chef's table, this time for supper. The bodyguards stepped aside to let Kara pass, but kept a watchful eye on her lest she try something again.

Kara stood at the edge of the table. "Did you get Olivia out?"

"Please, sit." Kara obliged and sat down across from Vasha. "Olivia is in police custody, but it is off the books. As for getting her released, I wasn't able to secure that."

"What?"

"As she is being kept off the records, they are forgoing due process, and committing an illegal act. Even if they were to just let her go, it would in effect be acknowledging their illegal activity. All my inquiries went unheeded."

Kara gritted her teeth. "I thought you said you were going to handle this."

Vasha raised her eyebrow. "I said I would apply some pressure and see what I could find out. This is what I found out. I have about as much sway with psychics as I do with the weather. It is an unfortunate reality for ones such as ourselves who work outside the law."

Kara started tapping her feet on the floor. The headache was creeping its way through her skull, and she could feel it behind her eyes now. She rubbed her eyes and shook her head.

"What now, then? What can we do?"

Vasha put on her best look of concern, but it felt hollow to Kara. "I'm afraid we are at the mercy of the detectives that have her in custody. Unless they release her, or someone breaks in to rescue her, there's not much we can do."

Break in...? "That's it."

"Hmm?" Vasha mumbled, intrigued.

"I'm going to break into the police station to rescue Olivia."

4. THE THIRD EYE OPENS AS THE FANGS CLOSE

*V*asha smirked. "You're going to rescue Olivia?"

"That's right, no thanks to you." Kara got up from her seat.

"Oh, but if you leave now I won't be able to earn that favour you gave me."

"You haven't so far," Kara said. "What are you holding back?"

Vasha picked up a tablet from the table beside her and began tapping on it. "I wanted to wait and be sure of your conviction to our dear Olivia before showing you this." She passed the tablet over to Kara.

Kara took the tablet and looked at the image on the screen. It looked like a blueprint of something, and there was a red dot in the middle on one side. "What am I looking at?"

"A blueprint of the fifth floor of the precinct that is holding Olivia."

Kara was taken aback. After everything that she had been through and how unhelpful Vasha had seemed, she's now delivered something that would make rescuing Olivia a thousand times easier.

"Why?"

The Vampire's Vision

Vasha raised her eyebrow. "I told you I was going to help, did I not? I was not able to have her released, but I assumed you would continue undeterred, so I gathered this information under that assumption."

Kara glanced at the tablet, then back to Vasha. "Thank you, Vasha. I had you pegged wrong."

Vasha laughed with genuine mirth. "Don't change your opinion of me just yet. I'm not doing this for free."

At this point, Kara couldn't tell if Vasha was helping her just for the favour, or because she wanted to help Olivia, or both. "So, what's the red dot?"

"That is where they are keeping our Olivia. She is being held in an interrogation room rather than standard holding cells. The reason is the same as before: they don't have her on the books. There are no windows directly to the interrogation rooms, but there are a few nearby."

Kara looked over the blueprints, trying to glean a plan of attack or at the least a way to reach Olivia without being seen, but they might as well have been hieroglyphs. She couldn't make heads or tails of what to do.

"What would you suggest?" She asked Vasha.

"It all depends on how you wish to make your mark. Use your abilities and you could wreak a special kind of havoc, and escape with Olivia before anyone knew what to do with you. However, if there are psychics in the police force, and their numbers are plentiful, you might not make it too far. If you prefer to avoid injury or confrontation, then you could cause a distraction."

"What kind of distraction?"

"That's up to you to decide, but," Vasha stood up and moved over to Kara, and then pointed at the tablet, "here on the other side of the building is where the holding cells are. If you were to use your powers to break the locks, the prisoners could attempt an escape, drawing everyone's attention. Then, in the confusion, you could go through the window closest to Olivia and make your escape."

"But then there's a chance of a criminal escaping."

Vasha smiled and pat Kara on the head. "Oh my dear, that's the point." She went back to her seat and sat down again. "They'll all be caught before they can get anywhere, and besides, these people are only there for misdemeanors. The real criminals are taken to prison."

Kara couldn't help but think that Vasha was generalizing and assuming it wouldn't be an issue, but she didn't have time to care about what ifs. Olivia needed her, and this was the best option without fighting through a few dozen people with guns and psychic powers.

"Can this be printed off?" Kara asked.

"Why don't you just keep the tablet?"

"Are you sure? Aren't these expensive?"

"It's a trifle. They come out with new ones every few months. I'll just get the newest model."

Kara pouted. *Wish I had that kind of disposable income. I'm lucky to get clothes on the salary Mr. Montgomery gives me.*

Vasha called to one of her bodyguards and he grabbed a nearby backpack and handed it to Kara. She looked inside; it was empty save for vials filled with blood.

"Those are for Olivia. I'm familiar with your... peculiar tastes. She might need her strength back, so you can give her those."

Kara nodded and shoved the tablet into the backpack, zipped it up, and placed it over her shoulder.

Vasha lifted her glass. "To your success," she said with a smile.

Kara nodded and left the restaurant. She went to the police station, and along the way she had time to steel herself for what she was about to do. Despite being a vampire, what most fictional accounts considered automatically evil, she managed to stay out of trouble for the most part. Today she was about to assist felons in escaping to help her friend escape.

After the cab arrived in front of the station, she drew in a deep breath then let it out. *Let's do this.*

She left the cab and went to an alley just to the side of the station. She counted the number of floors, and the fifth floor just happened to be the top one. She took out the tablet from the backpack and looked at the blueprint on it. The alley corresponded to the side the prisoners were in. Kara looked up and could see small, grated windows on the fifth floor. That also meant that the adjacent alley was the one with windows next to the interrogation rooms.

Kara put the tablet away, watched the sidewalk and street for traffic, and when there was a slight moment of inactivity, she knelt down and used her vampiric strength to vault herself up the side of the building.

There was nothing to hang onto, so Kara had to grip onto one of the steel grates on the fifth-floor windows and use her powers to stabilize herself. From her vantage point she could see a lot more of the city than normal. The air seemed a bit cleaner this high up, and she could actually see the sun off on the horizon. She was in a precarious position, however, and there was no time to admire the view. If she lost her grip and couldn't focus in time, even she could be hurt from this height.

Kara pulled herself up to look inside the police precinct. She could see the various thugs and afternoon drunks locked up in the holding cells, biding their time for release or incarceration. There were also a few people in suits who felt out of place amongst the other rabble.

Where's James? Kara thought she would see the drug dealer she and Olivia had visited in the morning, but he was nowhere to be found. *Maybe he's also being interrogated.* Kara didn't ponder on the oddity for long. James was none of her concern, only Olivia mattered.

She made visual contact with the lock of the first cell. Kara concentrated on the metal of the cell and applied pressure to it with her mind. The metal of the lock was strong and she was having trouble crushing it. She held her breath and tensed her body to will the muscle in her head to work harder. She could feel the headache she had been trying to ignore coming back into focus and ruining her concentration.

Kara had to let go. She relaxed and let out the breath she had been holding in. She leaned off the side of the building, her hand steady on the steel beam of the window. She took a few deep breaths to push the headache away again. *Focus, focus! Olivia is counting on you.*

Kara released the concentration she was using to hold her steady on the wall, and directed all her thoughts towards breaking the lock. She could feel the metal shaking like her hand was directly over it. She placed one hand on her temple to force the headache away and as a visual for what she was doing.

The lock buckled under her psychic pressure, compacted inward, and broke off the door itself. The crushing metal sounded like a head-on collision. The prisoners jumped back from the noise, and all eyes focussed on the lock.

Oh, God, that was too hard. I don't know if I can do that again. Kara noticed the cell door squeaking on its hinges, and it made her facepalm. *Of course! I don't need to break the whole lock, just the hinges or the metal holding the door in place.* Kara moved her attention to the next cell. *Focus!*

This time Kara tried to push the door off its hinges. She pushed and pulled with the motion of her free hand, and it helped her focus, which she found surprising. *I thought it was stupid in movies, but it actually works… I hope nobody sees me, though.*

With one final push the cell door flew off its hinges and hit the wall. She did the same for the other cells in the room that she could see as the prisoners attempted their escape. Beyond the holding cells Kara could see police officers with their guns out, running this way and that. There were two exits to the holding cells, and the prisoners were trying both in an attempt to leave. They didn't spare any time pondering what strange phenomenon had broken the cell, and just used the opportunity given them. Some did stay in their cells though, either not wanting further trouble, or too scared to try to escape.

That should do. Quickly now!

Kara jumped off the wall of the precinct to the other building in the alley, and deftly jumped from wall to wall to move to the adjacent alley while staying at the height of the fifth floor. She made her final leap towards the last window, fifteen feet from the edge of the building.

With one hand she grabbed onto the edge of the window, and used her telekinesis to keep herself from falling off. She pulled herself up and peeked through the window to see officers running in hysterics and she could hear shouting in all directions. There was no one in the hallway of the interrogation rooms, as she'd wanted.

The Vampire's Vision

She lifted the window from the inside and tore off the mesh screen and threw it into the alley. She pulled herself into the police station, falling without grace in a heap on the floor. She had to catch her breath for a moment. Using her powers was mentally exhausting. After a few seconds, she rose to her feet and went down the hallway to a large open doorway which led into the detectives' department.

Kara could see dozens of cops running around, guns out, shouting orders into the holding cells. She knew that, with their firepower, she wouldn't have long before they rounded up the escapees and came back to check on their other prisoners.

After making sure none of them were looking her way, she ran across the open doorway to the other side of the hallway. There were six interrogation rooms in the hallway, and Olivia was trapped in the third one from the back of the building where Kara had entered.

She grabbed onto the door handle and twisted the knob, but it was locked. She could feel sweat all over her face. At any moment, a cop could come walking around the corner and it would be over. She wiped her face and then gripped the knob again. She twisted hard, using her superior strength to break the lock meant to impede normal humans. She scanned her peripheral vision just in case someone had heard the noise. No one came. She opened the door.

Inside the interrogation room there was a man in dishevelled clothes, looking at her with concern.

"Whas goin' on out there?"

"Sorry, wrong room."

Kara pulled the door closed in one swift motion, then rushed to get the tablet out of the backpack again. After a quick check of the blueprint again, Kara shook her head.

Third from the front *of the building.*

Kara ran to the correct interrogation room and broke the lock like the last one. She opened the door, entered the room, and closed the door behind her.

Inside she saw the person she went through all this trouble for: Olivia.

"Liv!" Kara shouted, and ran over to her friend to give her a tight hug. Tears formed in her eyes as relief washed over her, and half of the stress that had piled up over the day fell away.

"You came," Olivia said in a weak, hoarse voice.

Kara pulled away from her embrace. "Of course I did."

She took a look at Olivia. It looked like they were torturing her. She looked tired, and there were several cuts on her face and arms, and small bruises elsewhere. Her cute clothes were torn, and a chunk of her hair was missing. Kara could also see something was off with her lips.

"Olivia, what's wrong with your mouth?"

Olivia looked away from her, shame written on her face. "Nothing."

Kara pulled Olivia's face back and made her show her teeth. Her left incisor was missing. Kara gasped and covered her mouth. "Liv!"

"Yeah, I know. Those bastards took out one of my teeth when I bit them."

Kara balled her fist in anger, and more tears washed down her face. "I'm sorry I didn't come for you sooner, Liv!" She embraced Olivia again, this time harder, and she winced in pain. "This is all my fault."

Olivia pulled away as best she could. "Hey, hey! That's not true. This is nobody's fault but the corrupt fuckers who did this to me," Olivia said, her strength and voice returning. "How did you get in here anyway?"

"We can talk about that later. We've already wasted enough time." Kara took off the backpack and took out the five vials of blood from Vasha.

"How…?"

"Vasha helped me," Kara replied.

Olivia gave Kara a wary look, but didn't comment on it. "I need your help. The detectives that were keeping me here used their powers to bind my hands, and I'm too weak to break it."

Kara looked at Olivia's hands on the table. She could feel the energy emanating from her wrists and holding her in place. She tried to probe and prod the binding, but she wasn't able to break it. She went over to the other side of the table.

"What are you doing?"

"I learned something earlier, and I think I can use it here. You know how in the movies when they show people with psychic powers waving their hands around as they move things with their mind?"

The Vampire's Vision

Olivia laughed. "You always said it looked stupid."

Kara chuckled and scratched her face. "Yeah, but I tried it today and it seems to work. I think I can use it to augment my normal strength as well. So, if I punch with my psychic powers aiding me, my punch will be stronger. I think I can break the binding on you if I do that."

"Are you sure this is safe?"

"Only one way to find out."

Kara lifted her fist up in the air, and gathered energy around her arm, wrist, and balled fist. After she had coated her whole arm she slammed it down on the table like a hammer. The table—which was also bolted to the floor—split in two with a thunderous noise like an explosion.

"Holy shit!" Olivia shouted.

Kara couldn't help but burst out laughing at the wreckage she'd caused. She had never felt such power in her fingertips before. She was weak by vampire standards, and always tried her best to avoid fighting.

The vials of blood had busted open on the floor from the force. "Damnit! Alright, come on Liv, let's get out of here before anyone checks on that noise."

Kara went over to Olivia, picked her up from the chair, and put her arm around her shoulder. Before they could even reach the door it opened and a man in a suit rushed in. He had a badge at his hip, and a gun drawn.

"Freeze!" he yelled, pointing the gun at them.

Kara focused on the gun and flung it out of the detective's hands and through the mirrored glass on the far wall. The gun broke through and shattered the glass.

The detective glanced from where the gun had gone over to Kara. He swiped his hand over, and a force pulled Olivia away from Kara. Olivia hit the brick wall and fell to the floor with a thud.

"Liv!" Kara shouted.

Kara's neck felt constricted like she was being choked, but there were no hands on her. She groped at air as she tried to remove the invisible constraints, to no avail. She looked at the detective to see him with his hand out like he was grabbing air, and she knew he was a psychic.

"I never thought I'd see the day when a psychic was friends with a vampire."

Kara struggled for breath, and used her powers to loosen his grip on her. "You don't know the half of it," she managed to squeak out.

Kara focussed and pulled the binding apart, but a real hand replaced the psychic one right after. The detective, Simmons by his name tag, was strong—too strong, in fact. He was using his powers to augment his strength, just as Kara had learned to do not a moment before. The difference was he was a full psychic who knew how to use his powers, and probably a stronger psychic than her anyway.

But he didn't know that she had the strength of a vampire behind her.

Kara gripped onto his hand with both of hers. She used her psychic abilities and her strength in tandem and ripped his hand off her throat. He came back and tried to grab her with both hands. She grabbed his wrists and the two struggled against each other for supremacy.

Kara gritted her teeth and pushed with all her might against Simmons. He pushed back with an equal force no normal human would have been able to muster. Kara protected her body with a barrier so he couldn't kick her. She could feel him attacking her wall with his mind, trying to overpower her as each second passed.

It was a standstill, but she could tell that he was the stronger psychic. Despite the adrenaline masking the headache, she was still fatigued from not feeding, and she was mentally exhausted from using her powers so much. If it went on for long, she would lose, and then both she and Olivia would be captives.

Before Kara could think of a way to end the stalemate, Olivia appeared behind Simmons and bit down on his shoulder. Simmons let out a scream of pain. She drank his blood like her life depended on it.

Simmons didn't waste any time, and used his powers to pull her teeth out of him, then he threw her across the room again. Olivia fell to the floor again, and this time she was out cold.

Kara saw no other way around it; she had to use the one advantage she had on Simmons. Her fangs were the answer. *I can't. I can't take the blood of the living.* Kara could feel her strength waning. Any second now, Simmons would overpower her, and who knows what would happen to her and Olivia next. *I have no choice. I have to save Liv! I'm sorry Mom.*

She used Olivia's distraction to push herself forward and sunk her own razor-sharp teeth into his shoulder. He grunted as the teeth pierced his flesh, and his blood began draining away.

As the blood entered her body, she could feel her strength returning. It wasn't much, but it was there. The more she drained from Simmons, the weaker he became as well. She didn't know how fast vampires drained blood, but she knew it only took losing a couple of litres before a normal-sized human would pass out. Kara aimed for those two litres and drained Simmons as fast as she could.

She felt a rush of another wave of adrenaline creeping from her toes all the way to the tips of her fingers. As the feeling of raw power flooded her body, she felt something else, something she had never felt before.

She could feel memories that weren't her own invading her consciousness. She closed her eyes, and an image appeared before her. She was looking through someone else's eyes. Flashes of images from the new perspective rushed through her mind along with words in a voice she was unfamiliar with, but at the same time it felt like her own.

She was looking at papers, a rap sheet... no, it's called a criminal record. "We got you on several counts of drug dealing, Mr. Moore," the voice said, and then faded away.

A new image was quick to replace the last, and she could see the druggie Olivia got brought in with. "I'll do whatever you say, just let me go," he pleaded.

Pathetic... But perhaps we can use him for something, Kara thought. Or was that even Kara's thought? She was unsure what her own thoughts were or who she was right now.

A new image appeared. It was James again, but this time in a cop car. She knew it was further in time than the last image. "Remember, two-thirty-four Strike Street," Kara said, or Simmons said.

Two-thirty-four Strike Street? That's where Raymond and the others live. Kara knew that was her own thought.

Before she could see any more images, Simmons' body fell to the floor in a heap. Kara opened her eyes to see Simmons passed out beneath her feet. Blood was dripping off her chin, she was shaking, and she felt sick to her stomach.

What did I just see?

Kara lifted her hands and stared at her palms, trying to ground herself back in reality. It was like she'd lost all sense of self in the span of a minute. One minute she was Simmons and the next she wasn't.

"Kara!" Olivia shouted. She ran over to Kara, and held her tight. "We have to get out of here."

Kara nodded as Olivia's warmth brought her back to reality. "Right. Uhh, there's a window I came in just down the hall," she said listlessly while pointing to the back of the building.

Olivia pulled on Kara's arm as she opened the door to the interrogation room. She glanced back and forth to check the hall, and then exited the room with Kara in tow.

The police station was still in chaos, with people shouting and loud, heavy footsteps stamping about. Outside, the sounds of a dozen different sirens filtered through the open windows, and a different siren was blaring inside the building as well.

Olivia went to the edge of the open doorway at one side of the hallway and peeked around the corner to see if the coast was clear. After being sure it was alright, she ran across. Kara followed behind at a close distance.

Olivia went to the open window missing the frame and stuck her head out. She examined the alley, and then came back inside. "You need to go first and then catch me with your powers."

Kara nodded, still feeling sick and not all there. Her stomach was aching and she was having trouble wrapping her mind around what had happened.

Olivia slapped Kara in the face, and it stung. She grabbed her face and gave Olivia a dirty look. "What the hell was that for?" she said in a harsh whisper.

Olivia smiled. "There you are. Now, jump down so you can catch me."

The Vampire's Vision

Kara nodded, this time with more vigor. She went to the window, climbed out, and jumped down. She did the same thing she'd done when Olivia tossed her from the fire escape, slowing herself enough that she could roll on the ground.

Her stomach churned as she rolled, and her sick feeling returned in spades. She looked up to see Olivia on the edge of the window. She motioned for Olivia to jump, and she did. Kara used her powers to slow Olivia's fall, but she caught her in her arms, and then let her gently down on the ground.

Olivia immediately went down the alley to get away from the police station, and Kara followed. Before they could get far, Kara had to stop.

Kara doubled over and threw up blood. She had consumed a lot of Simmons' blood, too much, and her body couldn't handle all that liquid that quickly.

"Kara, are you okay?"

Kara was breathing heavily and sweating, but she was able to rise to her feet with ease. "I'm fine, I'm fine," she stammered before giving Olivia a solemn look. "Liv, I think I can read minds."

Olivia was in shock. "Huh?"

"And I think Raymond and Damien are in trouble."

5. WRITTEN IN BLOOD

*Y*ou can what?" Olivia said.

"When I drank that detective's blood I... I think I could read his mind. It felt like I was him, and I could see his memories through his eyes." Kara stared at the pool of bile and blood on the paved gravel in the alley.

The sound of sirens and the red and blue lights blared into the alley on all sides. Olivia pulled out her wallet from her pocket and removed some single-serve wipes. She threw one over to Kara, and then opened one up for herself.

"We need to clean ourselves up and get out of here, and then we can talk more about what happened."

Kara looked at Olivia's bloody face and mouth, and she could feel the same blood drying on her face and chin. If anyone saw them as they were now, it would be difficult to explain. "Right," she replied.

Kara and Olivia both wiped themselves off as best they could, and then fixed their hair so they passed for competent but pale adult humans.

"How do I look?" Kara asked.

"Good enough. What about me?"

"Great, for the most part." The two of them had a laugh. "Hey, how did you have your things on you? Wouldn't they have taken that when they brought you in?"

The Vampire's Vision

"If they had of put me in one of the holding cells I imagine they would have, but they threw me into an interrogation room right away, and because of James they didn't get me registered into the police system. It probably would have been hard to register my belongings without who they belonged to, or they could just be lazy pricks. They did take all my cash though, including what was meant for Vasha from James' safe, the bastards." Olivia took one last moment to pull her hair back into a ponytail, and then turned around. "Come on, let's go."

Along the way back to Olivia's place, Kara asked her why they had been torturing her, or if it was just for some kind of twisted amusement. Olivia said that they were trying to get information on Vasha after they found out that she worked for her. She was lucky to lose only one of her incisors over it.

After arriving at Olivia's apartment, Olivia went to her washroom to take a look at herself and fix everything as best she could. Kara went straight to the couch, dropped the backpack to the side, and flopped down in it. She was exhausted, mentally and physically, from everything that had happened.

"God damn it, this stinks," Olivia shouted.

Kara opened her eyes and could see Olivia looking in her mirror. She was in varying states of smiling and was examining what she looked like with the missing tooth.

"If I see that detective again, I'm going to do more than drain his blood."

"Gideon should be able to fix it for you," Kara said.

"Yeah, I know," Olivia replied. "At least Vasha will cover the expenses."

After brushing her hair again and fixing herself as much as possible, Olivia went to her room to change. She came back out with a green tank top and new jeans on. She went to the couch and sat right on top of Kara.

"Oof," Kara grunted when Olivia landed.

"Am I too heavy for you?" she said with a devious smile.

"Yes," Kara replied, sticking her tongue out.

Olivia's jaw dropped in mock horror. "You little brat," she said as she pushed her friend's shoulder.

Olivia got up and the two sat beside each other. Olivia leaned over and gave Kara a hug. "Thank you for saving me, Kara."

"Was there ever any doubt? I know you'd do the same for me."

"Of course."

The two sat in silence, resting for a brief moment while they had the chance. It had been a long day for both of them.

"So, you can read minds now?" Olivia asked after a few minutes.

"I don't know. It was an odd experience to say the least. I saw images flashing through my mind, and when I closed my eyes it was like I was looking through someone else's. I realised that it was Simmons because he was talking with James, the person we met this morning. He gave him the address of Raymond and the others. I don't know why he gave James the address, but I doubt it was for something good."

"We should warn them about it," Olivia said.

"You can, I'm going to sleep. I did nothing but run around all day to save you." Kara closed her eyes and leaned back in the couch.

"I know it must have been hard for you, to take blood from the living again."

"He deserved it. Besides, I'm sure he'll survive. He seemed like a stubborn one."

"Just like every man," Olivia chuckled. "Thank you, Kara. I don't know how I'll ever repay you."

"I told you not to worry about it. If you want to you can buy me and Raymond supper at Kalie's."

"Kalie's?" she shouted with a big grin on her face. "We haven't been there in forever. I'll get their meatball Sammie," she stated with an excited fervor. "God, I loved that place. Why haven't we gone there in so long?"

Kara opened her eyes to give Olivia a skeptical look. "Because you're the only one who likes the food." She sat back and closed her eyes again. "Raymond helped me out in confirming you were in the police station, so I told him we'd all eat there."

"Geez, you travelled all over the place, didn't you?"

"Mmm-hmm," Kara replied.

"You even went to see Vasha. What did you think of her?"

"She is everything that you said she was and more. Did you know that she can suppress psychic powers?" Kara asked, eyeing Olivia.

The Vampire's Vision

Olivia raised her brow. "Really?" Kara nodded. "That's impressive. I wish she would show me, maybe then you wouldn't have to come to my rescue." Olivia smiled. "So, she helped you out? How?"

"She gave me a tablet with blueprints of the precinct and your location on it, as well as those vials of blood we lost."

Olivia sat up straight. "Where's the tablet?"

"In that backpack," Kara replied, pointing at the bag on the floor.

Olivia reached inside the backpack and pulled out the tablet. She faced the camera downwards on her lap, and then motioned to Kara to be silent. Kara raised her brow, confused by Olivia's request.

"Aww, it's broken. It must have been damaged in your fight with the detective," Olivia said, making Kara more confused. Olivia tore the tablet apart like paper. The screen shattered and the circuits became exposed.

"Liv what—?" Kara started, but Olivia once more motioned to stay silent, this time with more urgency.

Olivia took the tablet and threw it into her fireplace. Then she doused it with kerosene and threw a lit match inside, making it burst into flames. After a few moments, the heat rose and the tablet began melting. Olivia went back to the couch and sat back down.

"Do you mind explaining what that was about?"

"You're too trusting, Kara. Vasha probably bugged the tablet."

Kara's eyes widened, but then she nodded. "Given what you've told me about her, that does make sense. Still, I was going to use that to play games," Kara said with a pout.

Olivia snickered. "You can play Candy Crush on your phone."

"Why would she bug the tablet? What could she find out about me that she doesn't already know?"

"I've seen her use the information she gets as blackmail, or to find information on who you care about, that sort of thing."

"Why do you work for her if she's like this?"

"I never said she was a saint. It pays the bills, and even though she can be manipulative and kind of a bitch sometimes, she's got connections we just don't have. If you're on her good side, it's far more beneficial than the other way around."

Kara wanted to tell Olivia about how Vasha was just going to leave her to rot, but no matter how she thought of phrasing it, she felt it would result in an argument.

"You look like you have something to say."

Kara shook her head. "No, no."

"C'mon Kara, spit it out. I already told you, she's just my employer. You're my friend." Olivia placed her hand on Kara's leg and gave it a squeeze.

"Vasha only helped me because I offered her a favour. Otherwise she was just going to leave you in the precinct."

Olivia groaned and got up from the couch. "Kara, now you owe her a favour? That was the worst thing you could have done." Kara didn't say anything. She just looked sheepish as Olivia paced the room. "She might force you do something illegal so that she can use it for blackmail afterwards. Ugh!" she shouted with a stomp of her feet. "There's nothing we can do about it now, we'll just have to cross that bridge when we come to it."

"Sorry," Kara squeaked.

Olivia went back to the couch. "No, it's not your fault. You were concerned about me. I can't be angry about that. For now, let's get some rest and we'll figure out what to do with James and whatever errand that detective sent him on. I'm texting Damien to be on alert and that we'll talk to them about why tomorrow."

"Good. Finally," Kara croaked, lying out on the couch again.

"You're going to stay the night?"

"If that's alright with you."

"Of course it is, but don't sleep on the couch. Sleep in my bed."

"Yay! Thanks Olivia," Kara said with a smile.

The two went into Olivia's room and slept soundly after the long, arduous day they had. The next morning, they went to Vasha's restaurant to see if she could help in finding James.

Olivia entered first, with Kara following behind her. Olivia waved to the bodyguards and they waved back with big smiles on their faces, until they noticed Kara.

"Where's the boss?"

"She's in the kitchen, Olivia. Nice to see you safe, we were worried there for a bit."

"No little psychic detective is going to keep me down, but if it wasn't for my friend Kara I'm not sure what would have happened. You must have met Kara, right?" Olivia motioned towards Kara, who grinned and waved to the bodyguards.

"Yeah, we've met," they replied with wary looks.

Olivia peered at the guards, then at Kara, and then walked past them. As they headed to the kitchen, she leaned in and whispered to Kara, "What was that about?"

"I may have had to bind them when I first showed up to speak with Vasha. It could have hurt their pride a bit." Olivia laughed, and Kara joined in.

They were still smiling when they entered the kitchen, where they could see many different chefs and cooks working away at stoves and ovens, shouting orders and preparing for the lunch rush. In the corner of the kitchen they could see Vasha, working alone, with her hair tied in a low ponytail.

Olivia and Kara weaved their way between the chefs and cooks to Vasha, and as they approached her she was wiping her hands off. She turned towards them with a bright smile on her face.

"Olivia my dear, so glad to see you safe!" she shouted above the din. She pulled Olivia in and gave her a kiss on either cheek.

"Vasha, it's so rare to see you in the kitchen these days. Is there a special occasion?"

Vasha looked at Olivia as if she had two heads. "Of course there is: you're back." Olivia and Kara were both dumbfounded. "I'm preparing your lunch," she said simply.

"Oh," Olivia replied.

Vasha looked disappointed. "You do not seem enthused."

"Well, it's just that we have important business. I wish we could stay and eat, but we won't be able to."

"Ah, I see. Well, what is this important business you need to attend to? If you've come to me, I assume you need my help?"

Kara was shocked. Vasha was acting like a completely different person now that Olivia was here. She'd felt like a viper ready to strike the other day, and now she was giving off the air of an old friend or motherly figure. Kara was still wary and tense. Even the thought of a conversation with Vasha sparked her fight or flight response. *How can I trust someone who acts so differently person to person?*

"Yes, we have reason to believe that the psychic detectives holding me hostage sent James Moore to attack a house some of our kind are living in. We need your help locating James so we can find out why the detectives sent him and to stop him from attacking our friends."

Vasha looked away in thought. "And how was it that you came across this information?"

"I overheard them interrogating him in the room next to mine," Olivia lied.

Vasha gave Olivia a look similar to the one she gave Kara the other day to kill her powers. "I know when you lie, Olivia," she seethed.

Olivia glanced back to Kara, looking for permission, or guidance. Kara nodded. She turned back to Vasha. "Kara read the detective's mind."

Vasha leaned on the kitchen's counter and peered at Kara. "I learn something new about you every day, it seems. Fascinating," she said in the same ecstasy-ridden tone, sending chills down Kara's spine again. She couldn't be sure, but she thought Olivia shuddered as well. "So, I will say to you what I said to young Kara here the other day: I gain nothing by helping you, so why should I?"

There was a slight pause before Olivia said, "Consider it a favour, and I'll owe you one in return."

"Liv!" Kara shouted.

"You already work for me, so a favour has no meaning," Vasha replied curtly.

Kara pursed her lips, took a breath, and stepped forward. "What about another one from me? Now that I can read minds I'm much more useful."

Olivia gave Kara a dirty look, but she just shrugged her shoulders.

"While that is tempting, I've found it difficult to force people into favours in bulk. They usually never accept the actual number owed. It's easiest to keep it to just one." Vasha went back to chopping vegetables, obviously checking out of a conversation that now bored her. "I'm afraid, my dears, that I won't be able to offer my assistance at this time."

While Vasha's tone was light and conversational, Kara felt an undertone of distaste which forced all thoughts of rebuttal from her mind. She believed that if they pressed further they risked the viper striking them.

The Vampire's Vision

Olivia and Kara apologized, and then left the premises in a hurry. They were on their own to find and stop James before he did who knows what to their friends.

6. BITING WORDS

"Well, what now?" Olivia asked outside the restaurant.

"We either have to find James, or tell Raymond, Damien, and the rest about the attack and prepare at the house."

Olivia had her lips pursed in a pensive look. "Maybe we should split up. You see what you can find out about James, and I go talk with Damien and the others."

Kara frowned. "I get what you're trying to do, but I don't need protection from Damien and the other vampires. I've had to deal with who I am for my whole life, and there's nothing they can say that they haven't said already."

Olivia had a sad look on her face. "Alright, as long as you're sure."

"I'm sure. It's like you've always said, I'm not weak. I can take whatever they throw at me. Let's go prepare for the attack with them."

As Kara and Olivia travelled to the vampire house they tried to come up with the best way to explain what they'd found out. They concluded that they would try the explanation they used on Vasha again, as the other vampires wouldn't be as perceptive as she was.

After arriving at the house, Olivia went up and knocked on the door. After a moment, Damien answered. When he opened the door and noticed Olivia his eyes lit up and his face softened into a smile, until he noticed Kara at her side.

The Vampire's Vision

Damien ignored Kara. "Olivia, you're alright." Damien stepped forward, but Olivia put her hand out to stop his approach.

"Did you get my text?"

Damien stepped back, flustered. "Uhh, yes. Why should we be on watch? Did something happen?" he asked, glancing from Kara to Olivia. "Kara didn't tell me what happened to you the other day. Does it have something to do with that?"

"Don't worry about that. Now, be a good boy and gather your housemates. They all need to hear this."

He nodded. "Right. I'll be back in a bit."

He ran up a set of stairs towards the rooms on the second floor. The house had six people living there, including Raymond and him. They were all vampires like Kara and Olivia, and they'd all known each other for years.

Kara and Olivia entered the main hall and waited for Damien to return with the others. After a few minutes he came back with Raymond and the other roommates. They were questioning each other about what was going on, and giving Kara angry glances.

"Alright, what was it you found out?" Damien asked.

"We found out of a possible attack that's going to happen. A psychic gave your address to another psychic for an unknown reason. We think that they want them to attack you, maybe even kill you all."

Damien and the other vampires were in disbelief. There hadn't been a concentrated attack on vampires in years.

"Really?" was all Damien could spit out.

"Yes, really," Olivia replied.

"How many are coming to attack?" Raymond asked.

"We don't know, but we should prepare for the worst. We need to be ready for an attack at any minute. If there's a lot of them, they could combine their powers and... well... we'd be fucked. Luckily, we have Kara to back us up."

Damien and the other vampires stared at Kara, her hoodie drawn and hands in her pockets. Damien shook his head. "You can stay, Olivia, but... Kara has to leave."

Olivia sighed. "We don't have time for your bullshit, Damien. Our ancestors only survived against psychics by hiding, so if we're going to fight we need to use their power against them."

Damien's attempt at civility in front of Olivia quickly faded. "Tch, I'd rather die," he spat, staring daggers at Kara. "Just because you look like us doesn't make you one of us."

"Shut the fuck up, Damien!" Olivia yelled. Damien was about to say something else, but she clocked him in the face, sending him sprawling on the floor. She turned and pulled Kara out of the house. "Shows what we get for trying to help them. They deserve what's coming to them." She turned around and faced the house while walking backwards. "Serves you right, assholes!" she screamed before turning back around. "I can't believe you dated that guy. And to think he's after me now, the nerve."

Kara pulled away from Olivia when they reached the sidewalk. "We can't just abandon them, they're our friends," she said while wiping her eyes.

"They *were* our friends. That ship sailed a long time ago, Kara."

The door of the house opened and Raymond came running out. He had on a thick jacket and a laptop bag slung over his shoulder.

"Raymond, go back to the house," Olivia commanded.

"No, I want to help."

"You'll be more help in the house with the others if that's what you want to do. As for us, we're done. If you want to save yourself from getting killed, then feel free to tag along."

"Liv, we're helping them," Kara said with force behind her words. "I don't want them to die."

Olivia stared at Kara for a moment before turning away with a sigh. "Then what do you propose we do? If we wanted to fight, the only way to do it would be with their help," she said, pointing to the house.

"There's only one thing we can do right now. We have to stop the attack before it happens."

7. TEN MINDS ARE BETTER THAN ONE

*A*nd just how are we going to stop the attack before it happens?" Olivia asked while resting a hand on her hip.

"We find James and stop him before he can do anything."

"That's easy enough to say, but how do you expect to find him?"

Kara looked at Raymond and his eyes shot open. "I… I suppose I could ask around. Someone might know something."

"We can also check his place. He's probably not going to be there, but we might be able to find a clue about where he went."

"Well, I suppose that's a start," Olivia conceded. "Raymond, why don't you go back to my place and do your thing while Kara and I go to James' place to see what we can dig up?" Olivia took out her keys and gave one of them to Raymond.

Raymond accepted the key. "Right," he said with a nod of his head. "I'll see what I can find out."

Raymond went to his car and drove off, and Olivia and Kara went to James Moore's apartment. They went up to the third floor, and when they reached the top step Olivia put her hair in a ponytail in a mirror of the day before. They went over to James' apartment and tested the door. It was locked.

Olivia twisted the knob past the breaking point with ease, and the door opened. "I'll search his room, you search here," Olivia suggested.

"Alright," Kara replied.

Kara glanced around the room, seeing where to start in her search. There was a severe lack of personal effects, aside from electronics. *Well, his computer might be the best bet for now.*

Kara went over to the computer desk in the corner of the living room, and turned on the monitor. The computer was already running, and the fan in the back creating a small hum in an otherwise quiet room. After the light of the monitor brought images to the screen, she began looking through the files and folders. She searched for anything that might give her an idea of the places he frequented. She settled on checking his internet history, which included a multitude of lewd websites, gaming forums, and craigslist ads which seemed to be looking for weed. She also could see that he was an overly active social media user.

Kara clicked on one of the image sharing sites he frequented, and to her surprise it logged her in automatically as James. From there, she was able to see all the pictures he'd posted as well as his information available on the website, but it only listed the address she and Olivia were currently at.

Kara started looking at the photos he was posting, and then she burst out laughing in hysterics. "What an idiot!" she couldn't help but yell.

Olivia ran into the room with Kara still doubled over laughing. "What? Did you find something?"

"Look, look!" she replied, pointing at the screen.

Olivia went over to the computer and peered at the screen, her eyes squinted. Kara was staring at her, anticipating her reaction.

"Oh my God," she said while shaking her head.

"I know right? All this wondering about where he is, and all we had to do was look at his pictures. He should know better than to post a photo with GPS on."

Olivia grinned while still shaking her head. "Look at the caption as well: 'Getting ready to bust some heads with the boys tonight,'" she paraphrased. "It looks like if we want to stop this attack we need to act fast."

"Right, I'll look up the address right now. Can you call Raymond and see if he found out anything, or if he can tell us about the building we're headed to? It might help if we know what we're up against."

The Vampire's Vision

Olivia got on her phone and did as she was asked. Meanwhile, Kara looked up the address and found that it was an old abandoned warehouse. Looking at it from the map service's street view, it looked fairly large and open.

Kara listened to the one-sided conversation for a few minutes, then Olivia said her goodbyes and hung up. "So...?"

"So, he said that James is gathering several psychics for a job, but wouldn't say what the job was. He's taking anyone until eight p.m. and then the job begins. James was being secretive about the meetup, and is only giving it out to people he knows, but we found that out easily enough."

Kara chuckled. "Yeah."

"Raymond looked up the address and said that for that type of warehouse there's a fire escape on both sides that leads to a second-floor catwalk, just like in all those action movies."

Kara lit up. "Oh, I know the ones he's talking about!" she shouted with a wide grin.

Olivia smiled. "He did caution that James and his company could be up there, though. He's going to meet us at the address in thirty minutes. That will give us a few hours before their planned time of attack."

"Let's get going then," Kara said.

Kara and Olivia headed to the warehouse, staying a few blocks away just in case they could be spotted. They texted Raymond to tell him where they were and he met them in his car a few minutes after they arrived.

"So, what's it like over there?" Raymond asked, pushing his glasses up.

"We're not sure. We didn't want to get close in case they had a lookout. Kara, can you sense anything?"

Kara peered down the street at the warehouse and squinted her eyes as she focussed. "I'm not sure. I sense a lot of psychic energy, but I'm not good enough to know how many people he has in there. I might be able to tell their locations as we get closer."

Olivia nodded. "Alright, let's get a closer look, but stay alert."

The others nodded, and then the three of them made their way towards the warehouse. As they approached, they couldn't see anyone guarding the main entrances, nor the visible fire escape for the second floor. They used their fleet feet to move in silence to the bottom of the fire escape, and then put their backs against the wall.

Kara closed her eyes and took a few deep breaths. "I can't sense anyone on the second floor," she whispered.

"Good, we'll be able to spy on them from there."

"It's like you guys have done this before," Raymond commented as the three made their way up the steel steps of the fire escape.

"It's been a while since the three of us have been together," Kara replied. "A lot has happened since then."

"Evidently."

Kara smiled, and they continued up the steps to a rusted old door. Olivia gripped the handle and turned the knob gently. It made no sound as she pulled the door open a crack to peer inside. After her inspection, she opened the door fully and nodded to Kara and Raymond. They entered the building and stepped onto a metal catwalk going around the perimeter of the warehouse. Olivia entered and closed the door behind her.

The three of them went to the edge of the catwalk, knelt down, and looked over the side to see twelve people lounging around on torn and weathered couches, or walking around and talking with each other. Lying on one of the couches and smoking something was James Moore. From where Kara and the others were they weren't able to hear anything, but knowing how many people there were was almost as much as they needed to know.

If this is everyone that's going to attack, then right now we're outnumbered by nine, and even with the others we're still outnumbered by four, Kara thought. "This is bad," she whispered. "We should leave and tell the guys. We can't take them on our own."

"We still need to find out their plan of attack. If we know that we can at least come up with a plan of our own," Olivia replied.

Kara furrowed her brow and deliberated over the issue in her head. The closer they got, the more they risked being seen, but Olivia was right. They needed more information, otherwise they would be dead in an instant.

The Vampire's Vision

Kara moved away from the catwalk edge, and then stood up and silently moved to the middle of the warehouse. Olivia and Raymond followed behind, creeping along so as to not make a sound.

The closer they got, the better they could hear the conversations that were going on. They could hear James complaining about the lack of people showing up.

"Has anyone gotten any messages?" James asked. He received a variety of negative answers. "Ugh, what a joke. I thought we could get at least twenty people."

"What did you expect, man? No one wants to hunt vampires anymore. It ain't cool," one of the men said.

"Look, this is an easy job. All we need to do is combine our powers and crush the house. No one will know what happened, and the detective said he'll make sure it's labelled as a structural issue."

"And then we get paid?"

James paused for a moment. "Yeah, after that you get paid."

The man looked James up and down. "Yeah, just like last time. This is why no one wants to show up no more, cause they know you ain't good for it."

"Yeah, no one wants ta help yer sorry ass anyways, getting beat by a buncha girls," another person said, which elicited laughter from some of those gathered.

"What did you say?" James shouted as he got up from the couch.

James walked over to the man who'd insulted him, and they went nose to nose. Each man looked like he was about to fight.

Maybe they'll take care of each other for us.

"Yeah, Moore, you wanna start something?" the man taunted as those around them gathered in expectation of a fight.

James was quiet, and the tension in the air was palpable, but it didn't seem to be escalating. Kara thought this would be a perfect opportunity, if only one of them would throw the first punch, or…

Kara used her powers to hit the aggressor in the stomach. He reeled back from the force, and James looked confused.

"You bastard," the man seethed.

James was backing away and holding his hands up. "No, no, no it wasn't me," he tried to shout, but the other man didn't seem to care.

They fought in a similar way to how Kara had fought with the detective—a fistfight, but while augmenting their strength with their psychic powers. Kara could feel that each of them were also trying to break through barriers the other person had up, but it was almost an even match in that regard. James was by far the weaker of the two physically, and would have been overpowered if not for his psychic abilities. He kept saying that it wasn't him and trying to back away from the other guy's attacks, but his 'friend' kept going.

When the two locked arms, Kara took another opportunity to push them into one of the spectators, and then moved the spectator's arm to hit another person. Soon enough those two were also fighting.

Kara kept taking opportunities to include more participants in the fight, and soon all but two of the people gathered were fighting with each other. She turned to look at Olivia and Raymond, who both had wide grins.

"Everyone, stop!" one of the people not fighting shouted. After a moment of non-compliance, Kara noticed him close his eyes and lift his hands to chest level.

As the young man lifted his hands, the fighters floated off the ground. They couldn't fight in the air, and their powers also seemed to be suppressed by that one man. After a moment he let them down.

"I thought this was a gathering of like-minded individuals, but I can see now that that is not the case. You are all a disgrace to psychics. I take my leave," he said in a distinct British accent.

He and another young man began walking away towards the opening of the warehouse.

"Wait, no, Simon, don't leave. We need you," James pleaded.

"Perhaps you should have thought of that before you started in-fighting. I think I've tired of America. Cheers," he said with a wave as he turned the corner of the warehouse. After a moment they could hear a car starting and speeding off.

"Damn it!" James shouted. "He was stronger than all of us combined. Without him this job will be a lot harder."

"This wouldn't have happened if you didn't start the fight," the man James fought said.

The Vampire's Vision

"I was trying to tell you that I didn't hit you, but you wouldn't listen."

"Then who hit me, James? Explain that."

James looked around to the others in the group. "Well, anyone want to fess up now? Who used their powers to hit him?" No matter who James looked at, they denied doing it.

Kara looked at Olivia and Raymond, and motioned for them to leave. As they were sneaking to the exit, they could still hear James and the others debating what had happened.

"Then, if no one here did it…"

Kara glanced over her shoulder, and she could see James concentrating. After a moment, he locked eyes with her.

"There!" he said, pointing at her.

"Run!" Kara shouted.

The three of them fled the warehouse. Kara could feel psychic blasts flying towards her as she reached the door. She jumped outside just as the force broke the door off its hinges with a loud snap.

Raymond and Olivia jumped off the stairs to the ground below, and turned around to make sure Kara was safe. Kara jumped over the railing and joined them on the ground, and they all ran towards Raymond's car.

Halfway to the car, the psychics ran out of the warehouse. Kara turned around just enough to send a wave towards them. Two of them stopped the wave, but it slowed them down just enough for Kara and the others to reach the car.

They jumped into Raymond's car and he threw the keys into the ignition. He turned the key and the car came to a start. He pumped on the gas, and the car went speeding away.

"Are they following us?" he asked.

"No, they've stopped," Kara replied from the back seat. "No, wait." Kara could see the ten of them standing side by side. She thought they had their eyes closed, and she could feel them gathering energy. "Oh, shit. You have to go down another street, now!"

"I can't, this is a straightaway for another kilometer," Raymond shouted back.

"Then go between the buildings," Olivia suggested, seeing what Kara saw, save the gathering energy.

Raymond was flustered. He glanced to his left and right. "I... I can't. They're too close together."

"Something's coming," Kara announced.

Olivia grabbed Kara's arm. "Make us go faster," she yelled.

Kara looked at her like a deer in headlights. "What?"

"Use your powers to make us go faster!"

Kara turned around to look at the back of the vehicle. She didn't even know where to begin to make the car speed up. "Step on the gas, Raymond."

"I am," he replied, frustrated.

"Floor it, damn it!" Olivia swore while she pressed on his leg.

The car picked up more speed as gas pumped into the engine faster. Kara closed her eyes and focussed on the back of the car. She remembered the psychic blasts the other psychics had sent her. She spread a force along the back of the car, and imagined that she was pushing against it. She could feel the car moving faster with her thoughts. It increased her confidence, and she pushed harder.

Kara opened her eyes and she could feel the psychic energy blast from the ten rushing towards them. The force was busting lampposts and churning up the street as it flew at them. If it caught the car, they would be sent flying, or worse. She glanced over her shoulder to see that they were close to the turn for the next street. *We might just make it.*

Raymond pulled on the wheel hard, and the car turned the corner. Kara tried to stabilize the car, but it was too unwieldy. She had to stop pushing the car forward, otherwise they would flip or head into one of the houses nearby.

Just as they crossed the threshold of the next street, the psychic wave hit the rear of the car. The car tumbled sideways. Kara's world turned upside down, flipped, and twisted again as the car fell into someone's lawn. It finally landed upside down after two full rotations.

Kara's head had been knocked around several times, and she felt nauseated, but otherwise she was alright. "Olivia, Raymond, are you guys alright?" she asked.

The Vampire's Vision

Raymond groaned. "I think I'm okay, but my glasses shattered and cut my forehead," he said, touching his forehead and pulling his fingers away to show blood on his fingertips. "It's shallow. It'll heal quickly."

"I'm good," Olivia replied.

Kara reached for her belt and depressed it, letting her fall to the roof with a thud. She stumbled around and opened the door of the car, then crawled out. She went to Olivia's door and opened it, then helped her out. Afterwards, Olivia went and helped Raymond out of the driver's side.

Kara walked away from the car in the direction of where the blast hit.

"Help me flip the car back over, Raymond," Olivia said.

While the two tried to flip the car, Kara was stumbling forward as her mind took in what she was seeing.

The psychic blast of the ten people had hit between two of the houses on the street they were on. The two houses were completely split in half, all the way through. She could see the remnants of the other halves strewn about on the upturned lawns. Wood, busted appliances, crushed furniture, everything a normal house would have was now lying in bits in the dirt.

This is their power? Kara fell to her knees. *How can we win against this?*

She began to understand just why the vampires of old had been afraid of psychics, and the fear they must have had. She understood it so deeply because she now felt that same fear.

She looked at her own hands, and recalled the power she'd felt in the police station. It seemed pitiful in comparison. *How can I even help in this fight?*

"Kara, get up!" Olivia yelled.

Kara couldn't move. Her legs wouldn't work. Olivia ran over to her and picked her up off the ground. Then Olivia noticed what happened to the houses as well. She missed a step, but regained it quickly.

"Now you can see why I bring you along all the time," Olivia commented.

Olivia opened the back door of the car and placed Kara inside, then went into the front seat. Raymond hammered the gas, and they sped off just as they heard the noise of sirens approaching.

"We're doomed."

8. PSYCHICS VS. VAMPIRES

W e're not doomed, don't be so dramatic," Olivia admonished.

Kara's eyes opened wide and she leaned forward in her seat. "Did you see what they did back there?"

"Yes."

"They're too powerful. Maybe in a one-on-one fistfight, if they didn't have a chance to bind anyone, then we could win. The ten of them together, with their powers combined..." Kara shook her head as she trailed off. "We're no match for that."

Olivia slapped Kara across the face. She was taken aback, and stunned into silence.

"Now you listen here, Kara, because I'm only going to say this once. We're stronger than them, you're stronger than them. You know why I know that? Because just the other day you broke into a police station, and while you were already exhausted you fought another psychic and won. I didn't lose one of my fangs just for us to give up when those bastards come knocking at our door, and you didn't risk everything just so you could run away when things got tough. You fought back, and that's what we're going to do now. End of story." Olivia turned back around in her seat and folded her arms. "Got it?"

Kara could still feel the harsh, throbbing pain on her cheek. She brought her hand up to her cheek and pressed on it to dull the sting. She smiled. "Thanks, Olivia. I needed that."

"You're welcome," Olivia replied, still in a harsh tone. After a moment she turned around and had a sad, concerned look on her face. "Are you okay? I didn't mean to hit you that hard. I'm sorry," she said with an exaggerated, yet still genuine, frown. She placed her hand on Kara's knee.

Kara laughed and gripped Olivia's hand. "I'm fine. I needed the wakeup. I know we can do this, I just don't know how."

"Yeah, neither do I," Olivia said with a chuckle.

"Well... I might have an idea," Raymond announced. "But we're going to need their help."

"Who?" Kara asked.

...

"So as you can see, guys, if we're going to make it through this, we need to work together just like they are. Otherwise, we're as good as dead," Raymond explained.

They had returned to Raymond and Damien's house to try to convince the other vampires to work with them again. This time Raymond headed the argument, with Olivia providing the details of the psychics' powers.

Damien glanced to the four other vampires, and they nodded. "Alright, we're in," he said. "But it's only to fight them. After that, she's not welcome." He pointed at Kara.

"Damien, stop being an ass," Raymond shot. "You can keep your opinions, no one's taking them from you, just keep them to yourself."

Damien pursed his lips and clenched his teeth, but didn't say another word. Raymond glanced over his shoulder at Olivia and Kara with a look of fear on his face, but they replied with a thumbs-up and an impressed look on theirs.

"So, what's the plan?" one of the other vampires asked.

Raymond cleared his throat and explained his idea. "Right, so with the thought of the psychics teaming up to use their powers together, the best plan of attack is to draw them away from each other. If we can separate them, then we can overpower them fairly easily. It's just getting to that point which is the hard part."

"So, how do we split them up?" Damien questioned.

"It depends on how they come to attack us," Raymond explained. "I figure there's only two ways it can go down. First, they could come by foot, which is the easiest for us. If we hide between the houses along the street, as they walk along we can use Kara's powers to bind them, then spirit them away one by one. It wouldn't be long before their numbers dwindle, then we can just ambush the rest."

"What's the hard way?"

"They come by car. If they're in a vehicle it'll be harder to stop them, and harder to pull them away. If they stay in the car, they could drive off, they could attack us from afar, or they could easily combine their powers. If they come by car, we need to cripple the car, and then wait for them to exit. Stealth is our best and only option, but thankfully it's what we vampires do best."

Kara stepped forward. "If they come by car, it'll have to be at least two vehicles, as there's ten of them. I can take out one of the cars."

Damien glanced at Kara with spiteful eyes. "I'll take care of the other one."

"And, if by chance there's a third, I'll handle it," Olivia offered.

Before they exited to take to the shadows, Raymond handed everyone earbud headphones with a microphone attached to the cord. He then set up a conference call so they could stay in communication with each other, but out of sight.

After everything was ready, they left the house and, in groups of two, hid amongst the buildings along the street. Raymond had told Kara and Olivia earlier about how there were quite a few abandoned buildings on their street due to the owners not being able to pay their mortgages. He pointed them out so that they could hide without notice next to them.

"Everyone in position?" Olivia asked through her mic while standing next to Kara. They were hiding in the bushes between two houses that gave them a good view of both ends of the street, but still provided them cover.

"Raymond and me are in position across from you, Olivia," Damien replied.

"'*Raymond and I*' dumbass," Olivia scoffed.

"Whatever," he shouted. "We're here."

The other groups reported in from farther down the street, and now they just had to wait for the attack to happen.

Olivia and Kara were kneeling down with their backs to each other as they watched opposite ends of the street, waiting for their marks to arrive.

Kara muted her mic, then reached over and muted Olivia's before returning to her watch. "I feel I have to thank you again, Liv," she said.

"What for?"

"For helping me out back there. I appreciated the confidence boost."

"Well, I know how you can get sometimes, especially when it comes to things like this."

"Things like this?" Kara questioned.

Olivia turned around for a moment to look at Kara. "Remember how we met?"

Kara raised her brow, confused, but then it hit her and she smiled. "I got into a fight but I didn't fight back, and of course I lost. You were there, but you didn't help me."

"That's right, because if you weren't going to fight for yourself, why should I have?"

Kara grinned. "But even so, afterwards you took my arm and scolded me, and then you taught me how to fight."

"I knew you weren't weak, so to see you give up a fight like that... I could tell something was holding you back and making you weak. I wanted to teach you that you could be strong... that you *are* strong." Olivia grinned as she looked at Kara over her shoulder.

Kara smiled and felt the twinge of a tear forming at the corner of her eye. She wiped it away. "I don't know if I ever told you why I didn't want to fight back," she began. "I didn't want to fight because I couldn't control my psychic powers, and I didn't want anyone to know about them. I was so pathetic," she said with a sad smile. "I was so afraid of letting people see my true self that I would rather get beaten up. You were the first person I felt that I could trust with who I really was. If not for you, I don't know who I would be right now. Thank you, Olivia."

Olivia pushed Kara. "I'm trying to tell you that you don't have to thank me, you dummy," she chided with a smirk.

Kara was grinning, until the two of them heard the noise of a car approaching. Kara turned around to look at the approaching vehicle.

She noticed only one vehicle, but she could immediately tell that psychics were in it. She could feel the psychic energy radiating off the people inside. *Only one car? That can't be right.* Kara pulled the mic up to her mouth and whispered "Does anyone see another car?"

"Is that them, Kara?" Raymond's voice came over the earbud.

"Yes, that's them, do you see another car?" she asked again.

"Repeat, is that them, Kara?"

The Vampire's Vision

Damn it, the mic is still muted! Kara unmuted the mic and confirmed the first car held psychics, and repeated her question. Luckily the car was moving slowly as they were no doubt looking for the right address.

"It's on the other side of the street, on this end," one of the vampires said over the conference call.

Kara and Olivia peered over the bushes to the other end of the street and saw the car in question. It was too far away for Olivia or Damien to attack. "I'll take out the car down the street. Damien, you get the one closest to us afterwards," she suggested.

"Got it," he replied.

Kara imagined her hand hovering over the hood of the farther car. She mirrored the movement of her imagined hand with her real one as she balled it into a tight fist. "Get ready," she said. She punched downwards with all the physical and mental strength she could muster, twisting her hand as she did so to imbue it with more power.

An unseen force crushed the car's hood. The engine and other components were smashed to bits and pieces flew away from the chassis. The impact of Kara's psychic punch, as well as the momentum of the car, caused it to flip forward and onto its hood with a crash.

Not to be outdone, Damien sprung out of the shadows and into action. In one swift motion he used the car's thrust and his vampiric strength to lift it from the front and perform a suplex on it. He smashed the car down onto its hood just like the other, causing a slight tremor in the surrounding area. Damien took a moment to catch his breath before jumping back into the dark.

"That's how it's done," he bragged, even though it was clear it took a lot out of him.

Kara and Olivia observed the vehicles. Even though they just suffered heavy damage, the roofs were still intact. *They probably used their powers to protect them at the last minute,* Kara thought.

After a moment, the doors opened and five people crawled out of each car. Kara could see James coming out of the driver's side of the car closest to her. "Where are you, you damn leeches?" he shouted.

"Alright, let's get them separated. If you attack, be sure to move to a new area right away to not get attacked," Olivia advised.

Olivia looked at Kara, and Kara nodded. Kara searched for a target. She was going to use James, but she wanted him to herself. *I'll make sure you pay for what you made Liv endure, but she can handle one of your friends.* She bound one of James' comrades and pulled him towards the bushes she and Olivia were hiding behind at a high speed. She pulled him through the thick, spiky branches, and straight towards Olivia. Olivia had reared back, ready to strike. She punched him square in the face, sending him flying back through the bush. He fell to the ground, unconscious from one thunderous punch.

Kara and Olivia jumped away from the bushes. Psychic blasts tore the green shrubbery to bits, but they were already gone. They moved behind the house to hide, and then ran farther down the street under cover of the shadows.

They jumped on top of one of the abandoned houses and lay down on the roof to watch. Kara counted the psychics and there were only four on the far side of the street. *One of the guys must have taken someone out.* The psychics were jumping at shadows and stayed huddled together.

"Come out, you cowards!" James yelled as his eyes flitted back and forth across the street.

A flurry of rocks chucked at high speed hurtled towards James' group. Their barriers protected them from the brunt of the damage, but they still howled in pain. Two of the psychics picked up the rocks with their minds and flung them back to where they'd come from, but no one was there.

More rocks, bigger this time, darted at them from another direction. One of the stones hit a psychic in the jaw. He shouted an obscenity and ran in the direction the rocks came from.

"No, don't separate! That's what they want, damn it!"

James' words fell on deaf ears, and the psychic went around the corner of one of the houses. A second later he tumbled backwards towards the street before falling flat on his face. He wasn't moving.

James gritted his teeth and began searching the shadows more fervently.

Kara glanced over to the other car, and the other group of psychics had lost another man. Now there were three psychics on each side of the street.

We might just be able to win.

Kara looked over at Olivia and caught her attention. "Let's go in for another attack and end this," she suggested.

Olivia nodded, and the two of them began standing up on the roof. "Got you!" Kara heard, turning her attention back to James' group.

Raymond was floating in the air, clutching his neck. James had his hand out in the shape of a claw, like he was choking the air. Kara's instincts kicked in and she moved to get up. Olivia gripped her arm and stopped her from leaving. She gave Olivia a dirty look, but stopped just in time to see Damien running out of the shadows.

Damien rushed towards James, his fist cocked to strike. Damien went for a powerful punch right to James' jaw, but froze in place inches before contact. The other two psychics had stopped him.

James laughed maniacally, and then slammed his hand down. He tossed Raymond down to the pavement face first. Raymond's face broke on the concrete and stone and his glasses shattered to pieces.

Olivia let go of Kara's arm. "Raymond!" Kara shouted as she rose to her feet on the roof.

Kara gritted her teeth in anger and leapt from the building with all her strength. She sent a blast of energy at the two psychics pinning Damien. Their bodies collided violently with the car behind them, and they lost their hold on Damien. Damien's momentum was stunted, and he stumbled forward, catching himself before he fell. Still in the air, Kara reared her arm back, coiled her hand into a fist, and coated it with power.

James lifted his hand to stop her with his mind, but before he could pull his thoughts together Damien was behind him. Damien wrapped his muscular arms under James' arms and around his neck, putting him in a full nelson. Damien then lifted him off the ground towards Kara's collision course.

Kara let out a guttural yell like a lion's roar, and thrust her fist towards James. His face contorted in fear and pain even before the fist made contact. Her punch hit and there was a violent explosion of air. The force of the impact sent James and Damien back twenty feet. They hit the ground and rolled several times before stopping in the middle of a grassy lawn.

Kara landed on her feet, stepping forward a few times before she could control her momentum. She glanced to her right to see the two psychics knocked out and Olivia right there next to them. She was panting, but not the worse for wear. She looked to her left and then ran over to Raymond to check on him. Kara's eyes followed Olivia, and then her feet made to do the same. Olivia turned Raymond over and checked his pulse.

"He's alright," she said.

Kara checked the other end of the street, and could see the other vampires had already won their fights. All the attackers were defeated.

"Go check on Damien," Olivia said.

Kara nodded, and then ran over to where Damien had fallen. "Damien! Damien, are you alright?" she asked as her voice cracked. She turned him over and held him in her arms. He had scrapes and bruises all over his body. His eyes were closed, but she could tell he was breathing. "Damien," she called again, shaking him.

He opened his eyes slowly. "I'm here, I'm here, God." He sat up and brushed himself off.

"I'm so glad, I was worried," Kara said, tears forming in her eyes. She turned away from Damien when she noticed them and wiped her face. "Sorry," she muttered.

Silence pervaded the area, and tension rose. Damien scratched his head. "That's one hell of a punch you threw there. Have you… have you been working out?"

Kara chuckled and turned around as she finished wiping her eyes. "No, I just recently learned how to do that." Kara wasn't sure in the dark of the night, but she thought that she could see the faintest hint of rosiness around Damien's ivory cheeks.

"Well, I'll keep it in mind next time I need a sparring partner," Damien mumbled.

Kara laughed, but deep down she hoped he was serious. "Oh!" she cried, springing to her feet.

Kara ran over to where James was lying on the ground. He was knocked out cold, and she could see a red welt on his jaw from where she'd punched him. She hoisted him over her shoulder and walked back over to where Olivia and Raymond were.

Raymond was just getting to his feet with Olivia's help. "Are you alright, Raymond?" Kara asked.

"I'll be fine, but my glasses have seen better days," he replied with a slight lisp from an already swollen lip. His face was scraped and bloody, but it was nothing that wouldn't heal.

"Who's that you have over your shoulder?" Olivia asked.

"James Moore," Kara replied with a smile. "We finally got him, and now you can take him back to Vasha."

Olivia smiled. "Right on!" She raised her hand and gave Kara a high five. "Hey Raymond, can I borrow your car so I can take him to Vasha's?"

"Sure," he replied.

"What do we do about the other psychics?" Damien asked.

The Vampire's Vision

Before Kara could answer, they heard the sound of blaring sirens approaching from afar. "I think we have our answer," she said. "Just lay low for a while, and everything should be fine."

"We can hide out in one of the abandoned houses until the police leave," Damien said. "We might need to move soon though, since those damn… since the psychics seem to know where we live anyway."

Olivia handed Raymond over to Damien. "Let us know if you run into any more trouble."

Damien nodded and walked away with Raymond in tow. "Talk to you soon," he said.

Kara couldn't be certain, but she thought he might have been extending that to her and not just Olivia. The thought brought a smile to her face, and warmth to her chest despite the cold of the night.

Olivia gave her a gentle nudge and a knowing glance, and they shared a smile together.

The two of them put James in the back seat of Raymond's car and drove to Vasha's. "Well, this is it. You coming in with me?"

"No, I'm going to catch a cab and go home. I'm dead tired."

Olivia laughed. "Alright, talk to you soon." Kara started to get out of the car, but Olivia stopped her. "What about Kalie's?" she asked with an urgent look in her eyes.

Kara chuckled. "I promise we'll get a meal at Kalie's tomorrow as long as Raymond is up to it."

Olivia pumped her fist. "Yes!"

Kara laughed, and the two exited the car. She waved goodbye to her friend, then waved down a cab and took it to her home.

As soon as she entered, the familiar smells and sights brought joy to her heart. She had been through a lot over the past couple of days, and the weight of it all lifting from her shoulders made her feel new again.

"Kara! Kara, is that you?" an elderly voice rang out from one of the rooms.

"Yes, it's me," she replied.

Before long, Mr. Montgomery shuffled out from the back of the apartment. When he saw Kara in the flesh his face lit up with relief. He pointed his cane at her.

"You had me worried sick! You haven't been home for a whole day!" He looked her over. "And what happened to you? You look like you've been through the wringer."

Kara made her way to the couch and lay down in it. "It's been a long couple of days, Mr. Montgomery. I'm sorry I worried you," she said with a yawn.

The old man's face softened. He moved closer to the couch. "Did you find your friend?"

"Yes, she's safe now. Everything's over…" She trailed off as she fell asleep right there on the couch.

"Dumb girl, can't even get in her own bed," Magnus muttered.

He eyed Kara for a moment, then grabbed a blanket and placed it over her before mumbling about how ungrateful she was as he headed back to his room.

Kara slept soundly that night, better than she had in many moons. She hoped that that would be the end of fighting against psychics and using her powers, but little did she know that this was only the beginning.

THE END

THE VAMPIRE'S RESCUE

Book 2 of Shawn Wiseman's debut series

PSYCHICS VS. VAMPIRES

Is on sale now through Amazon, Print and Digital.

ABOUT THE AUTHOR

Shawn Wiseman credits his love of reading and writing to his parents, who taught him how to read from an early age, and fostered his creativity.

After almost becoming a boring businessman, Shawn decided to try his hand at writing, and found his passion. He likes strong characters, lots of action, and punchy dialogue. Some of his vices include video games, swearing like a sailor, and fast food.

Shawn gets inspiration from his friends and family who continue to encourage him with his writing. Before trying his hand at self-publishing, a friend was the one who convinced him to try a writing challenge, and he hasn't looked back since then. His biggest goal is to create characters and stories that will inspire others to try their hand at writing, just as he was inspired before.

It would help Shawn out if you shared this novel with your friends or leave a review on Amazon.